Animales pequeñitos / Itty Bitty Animals

RANITAS PEQUEÑITAS/ ITTY BITTY TREE FROGS

By Gunner Quick   Traducción al español: Eida de la Vega

Please visit our website, www.garethstevens.com. For a free color catalog of all our high-quality books, call toll free 1-800-542-2595 or fax 1-877-542-2596.

Library of Congress Cataloging-in-Publication Data

Quick, Gunner.
Itty bitty tree frogs = Ranitas pequeñitas / by Gunner Quick.
  p. cm. — (Itty bitty animals = Animales pequeñitos)
Parallel title: Ranitas pequeñitas
In English and Spanish.
Includes index.
ISBN 978-1-4339-9913-0 (library binding)
1. Hylidae — Juvenile literature. 2. Tree frogs. 3. Frogs. I. Title.
QL668.E24 Q53 2014
597.878—dc23

First Edition

Published in 2014 by
Gareth Stevens Publishing
111 East 14th Street, Suite 349
New York, NY 10003

Copyright © 2014 Gareth Stevens Publishing

Editor: Ryan Nagelhout
Designer: Nicholas Domiano
Spanish Translation: Eida de la Vega

Photo credits: Cover, pp.1, 5, 9, 13, 19, 23, 24 (feet, leaves) iStockphoto/Thinkstock.com; p. 7 Heiko Kiera/Shutterstock.com; p. 11 Eduard Kyslynskyy/Shutterstock.com; p. 15 Bianca Lavies/National Geographic/Getty Images; p. 17 Brandon Alms/Shutterstock.com; p. 21 Photodisc/Thinkstock.com.

All rights reserved. No part of this book may be reproduced in any form without permission in writing from the publisher, except by a reviewer.

Printed in the United States of America

CPSIA compliance information: Batch #CW14GS: For further information contact Gareth Stevens, New York, New York at 1-800-542-2595.

Contenido

Ranitas diminutas. 4

Pies pegajosos 12

Cambio de color 18

Palabras que debes saber 24

Índice 24

Contents

Small Frogs 4

Very Sticky. 12

Changing Colors 18

Words to Know 24

Index. 24

¡Las ranas de árbol son diminutas!

Tree frogs are tiny!

Viven en los árboles.

They live in trees.

7

Son muy ligeras.
Pueden moverse por
encima de las hojas.

They are very light.
They can move
on top of leaves.

9

Sus largas patas
las ayudan a saltar.

Their long legs help
them jump.

Tienen pies pegajosos que las ayudan a trepar.

They have very sticky feet. These help them climb.

A las ranas de árbol
verdes les encanta
comer moscas.

Green tree frogs love
to eat flies.

Las ranas de ojos rojos duermen durante el día.

Red-eyed frogs sleep during the day.

¡Las ranas de árbol grises pueden cambiar de color! Se pueden volver verdes.

Gray tree frogs can change color! They can turn green.

¡Algunas ranitas son muy tóxicas! Se llaman ranas venenosas de dardo.

Some are toxic! These are called poison dart frogs.

¡Sus brillantes colores
les avisan a otros
animales que no
se acerquen!

Their many bright
colors tell other animals
to stay away!

Palabras que debes saber/ Words to Know

(los) pies/
feet

(las) hojas/
leaves

Índice / Index

ranas de árbol grises/
gray tree frogs 18

ranas de ojos rojos/
red-eyed frogs 16

ranas de árbol verdes/
green tree frogs 14

ranas venenosas de dardo/
poison dart frogs 20